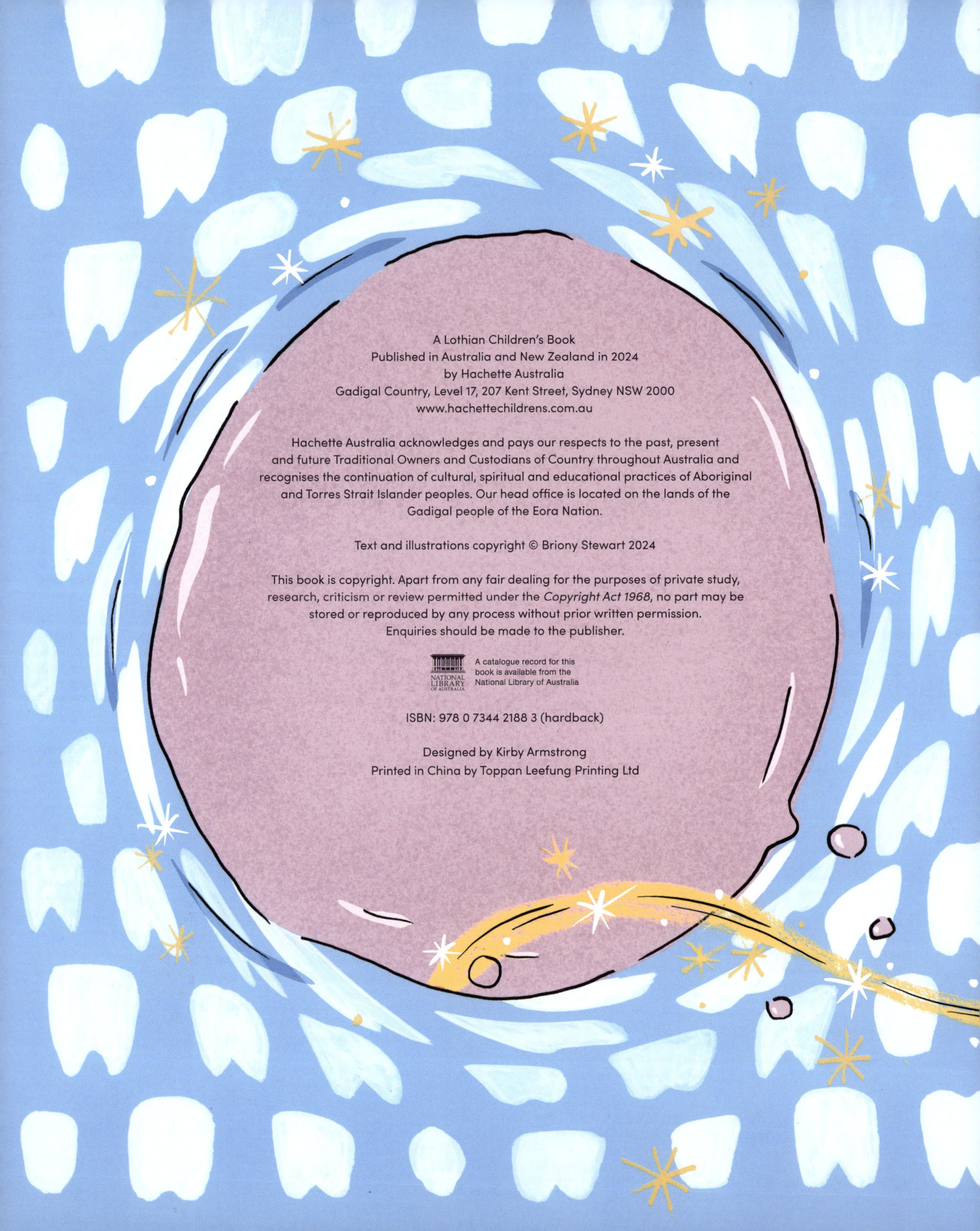

A Lothian Children's Book
Published in Australia and New Zealand in 2024
by Hachette Australia
Gadigal Country, Level 17, 207 Kent Street, Sydney NSW 2000
www.hachettechildrens.com.au

Hachette Australia acknowledges and pays our respects to the past, present and future Traditional Owners and Custodians of Country throughout Australia and recognises the continuation of cultural, spiritual and educational practices of Aboriginal and Torres Strait Islander peoples. Our head office is located on the lands of the Gadigal people of the Eora Nation.

NATIONAL LIBRARY OF AUSTRALIA
A catalogue record for this book is available from the National Library of Australia

ISBN: 978 0 7344 2188 3 (hardback)

Designed by Kirby Armstrong
Printed in China by Toppan Leefung Printing Ltd

Everything You Ever Wanted to Know About the Tooth Fairy (and Some Things You Didn't)

BRIONY STEWART

LOTHIAN Children's Books

Every single minute of every single day, a child somewhere loses a baby tooth. In fact, if you put all the children of the world together, they are losing more than 200 teeth a minute – that's 300,000 teeth every day!

You might be wondering what happens to all those teeth?

They are collected, of course,

by tooth fairies!

What's a tooth fairy?

This is a tooth fairy. It hopes you will never see it. It's only a little bit bigger than your thumbnail. People often think that there is only ONE tooth fairy, when really there are millions. Like us, they are all different, but in many ways they are also more or less the same.

Tooth fairies only have two teeth that they are born with and never lose

Soft, all-day pyjamas for maximum comfort. Why wear anything else?

Pocket to keep shrunken coins in

Wings for balance and steering (flying is powered by fairy dust)

Fairy dust bag

Socks for quiet sneaking and for looking stylish

What do tooth fairies eat?

Tooth fairies aren't picky about what they eat. Often it is a bit of whatever is nearest while they are waiting to collect a tooth. A bit of bark, a leaf … your dirty socks.

If you ever find a teeny-weeny chomp in something, it might have been nibbled by a hungry tooth fairy.

What do they do with the teeth?

It might sound a little revolting, but children's teeth are an important part of a tooth fairy's daily life. While a few teeth will be enlarged and turned into homes, schools and shops, most teeth are collected as a vital ingredient in a magical substance called 'fairy dust'.

Rotten teeth with cavities tend to leak a lot of their magic. They can't be used for houses or fairy dust, but tooth fairies still collect them. These teeth are crushed to make roads and walls, or to plant gardens in.

What magic do tooth fairies have?

Fairy dust is the secret to a tooth fairy's magic and it is used in just about everything they do.

Flying and floating

Growing and shrinking

Putting children back to sleep

Locating teeth

Lifting heavy objects

Making magic portals

Making music

Turning each other into toadstools just for fun

Why do tooth fairies like children's teeth?

In ancient times, tooth fairies would collect *any* kind of tooth. Dinosaur teeth, sabre-tooth fangs, woolly mammoth tusks ... But the magic from *these* teeth was almost as dangerous as the creatures they came from.

In time, tooth fairies discovered that human baby teeth were safer and especially powerful with good magic. These were teeth that had heard a first giggle, had uttered first words or had bitten into a strawberry for the first time. They were teeth that fell out gently before they ever tasted horrible things like coffee or a rotting Triceratops.

How do they take your tooth?

After completing training in advanced sneaking, coin embiggening, and tooth carrying, tooth fairies are skilled at crawling under pillows and hard-to-reach places to swap teeth for money.

They wait until dark, when they think humans will be sleeping.

They make a magic portal right into the house they need to visit.

If the coast is clear, they make the swap very quickly,

then carry the tooth back through the portal.

Where do tooth fairies live?

On the other side of those fairy-dust portals, tooth fairies live in small, hard-to-find villages in Hypnagogia (Hyp-na-go-gee-ah), also known as The Land of Waking Dreams. It is an enchanted place, halfway between our world and Slumberland, where magic can flourish.

This is what a typical tooth fairy village looks like.

What's inside a tooth fairy's house?

After popping up out of the Hypnagogian soil, baby tooth fairies are fully grown within a few short weeks. The first thing a grown-up fairy must do (after completing their tooth fairy training) is to build themselves a home, making a perfect space just for one. While tooth fairies live alone, they are never lonely because they are always visiting their neighbours and finding things to do in their busy, buzzing little villages.

Does the tooth fairy visit other countries?

Of course! Although in some countries, such as Korea and Brazil, children throw their teeth into the air to be collected by birds.

Other children in places such as France, Belgium and Morocco believe a little mouse collects their teeth.

Birds and mice are just some of the specially trained pets that help tooth fairies collect teeth.

Speaking of pets, tooth fairies often adopt dust bunnies. These are clumps of household dust that have been exposed to magic. It happens from time to time: a tooth fairy sneaks into a dusty house, uses a little too much magic and PING the dust springs to life! Some houses are running rife with these little floofs (you are not imagining it, they really can multiply like crazy).

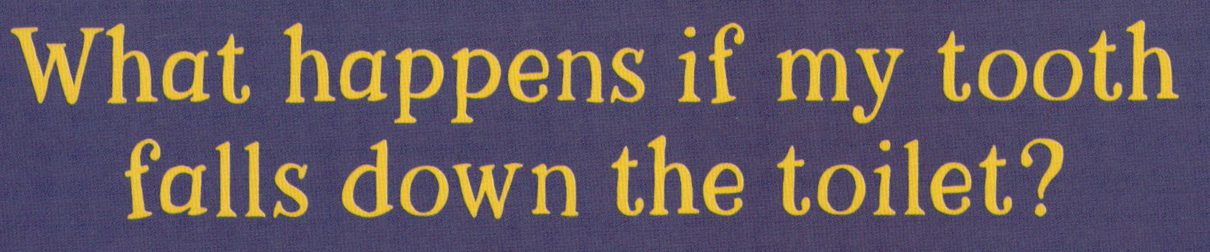

What happens if my tooth falls down the toilet?

(Or the drain, or I swallow it?)

Just as bees can find flowers, tooth fairies can locate teeth that have been dropped almost anywhere in the world! Even swallowed teeth reappear eventually . . . though the fairies generally don't want *those* ones anymore. But not to worry – the tooth fairy will always try to leave a gift for you anyway, so that you'll try again next time.

What happens if I want to keep my tooth?

Tooth fairies know that teeth are special. While they really want your tooth, if you are not ready to let it go they will still leave a gift for you and hope you might give them a tooth another time. They know that you will lose 20 baby teeth in your life and that eventually you will probably choose to give some of them away.

Why do tooth fairies give you money?

Stealing teeth is very risky. People do not want their teeth stolen. Most children will, however, willingly swap their teeth for gifts. But what kind of gift?

Interesting pebbles?

Funky socks?

Jars of chutney?

Children did not seem to enjoy these as much as the fairies thought they would.

Children *did* seem to like something called 'money' though, so this became a standard gift.

Where do tooth fairies *get* the money?

Tooth fairies are excellent foragers and gatherers. If they can find lost teeth, they can certainly find lost money. Beaches, storm gutters and sofa cushions are some of their favourite places to search. But that means you may want to wash your hands after handling the money. You never know where they might have found it.

Because they are small and money is heavy, they have to shrink it right down to a tiny size for carrying and storing. Once it is in the right position under a pillow, the money is returned to its normal size.

Why does the tooth fairy leave different amounts of money?

(or sometimes even forget to come!)

While tooth fairies might be good at finding human money, most of them don't really know what it is used for or how much to leave, so the amount can vary between households.

In addition to this, different tooth fairies visit each home. Some of them are very organised, while others are a little sloppy or downright forgetful!

Some leave tiny letters,

some leave glitter.

Some leave things
that look like chocolate
sprinkles but aren't . . .

No two visits are exactly alike.

How do tooth fairies know when you've lost a tooth?

Perhaps the most mysterious and least understood aspect of tooth-magic is this: When a tooth falls out it makes a spark, invisible to our eyes, but bright enough to appear in the skies over Hypnagogia. These star-like constellations, affectionately known as the Milktooth Way, are used by tooth fairies as a map. They follow the magic to wherever a new tooth may be.

Why do tooth fairies stay hidden?

If *you* were that tiny, would *you* want giants to know where you lived? Tooth fairies are fond of humans, especially children, but when anything from a dropped snack to a sneeze can be dangerous, being too close to humans is not advisable.

Why don't some people believe in tooth fairies?

Whether you believe in tooth fairies or not is up to you. Some people don't and that's okay. There are always enough teeth hidden under pillows for tooth fairies every night.

Older humans aren't losing baby teeth anymore and by staying hidden, tooth fairies hope that grown-ups will stop believing in them just enough to leave them alone. After all, people don't go looking too hard for things they don't believe in!

I lost a tooth! What should I do?

Celebrate! This exciting moment means that you are growing up!

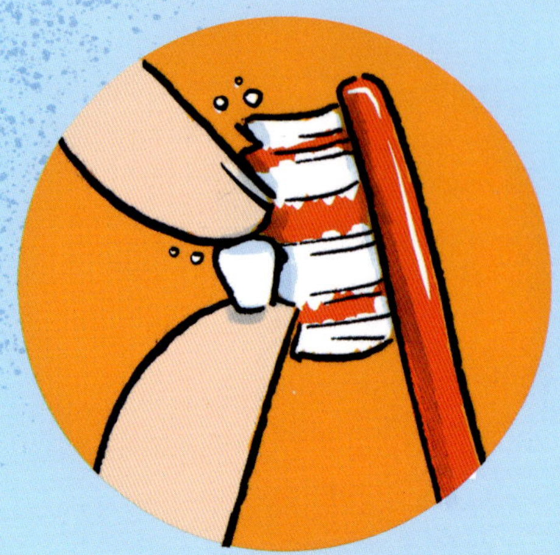

Give your tooth a little wash (careful, don't drop it, put the plug in).

Put it in a small bag or box and leave it under your pillow, perhaps near the edge so it's easier for the tooth fairy to reach.

Leave a friendly note if you feel like it.

Then, snuggle down, get comfy, close your eyes and ... wait!

Since losing her first tooth, Briony has been interested in the ways of tooth fairies. Growing up in the halls of the University of Western Australia's Zoology department where her father worked, Briony first began attempting to order fairies into taxonomic categories at the age of 9. Now an award-winning children's book author and illustrator, she is proud to study and document the whimsical world alongside her two children and biologist husband in Fremantle, Western Australia.